This one's just for Eilidh—T.N.

For Jake—S.H.

tiger tales
5 River Road, Suite 128, Wilton, CT 06897
Published in the United States 2021
Originally published in Great Britain 2017
by the Little Tiger Group
Text copyright © 2017 Tom Nicoll
Illustrations copyright © 2017 Sarah Horne
ISBN-13: 978-1-68010-219-2
ISBN-10: 1-68010-219-2
Printed in the USA
STP/4800/0390/1220
10 9 8 7 6 5 4 3 2 1

For more insight and activities, visit us at www.tigertalesbooks.com

THERE'S A
DRAGON
IN MY
POPCORN!

by TOM NICOLL

Illustrated by
SARAH HORNE

tiger tales

Contents

Chapter 1
AT THE MOVIES
7

Chapter 2
CALLING ALL FILMMAKERS
22

Chapter 3
EVERYDAY HEROES
37

Chapter 4
TOBY OR NOT TOBY
48

Chapter 5
WHO WANTS TO BE A STAR?
63

Chapter 6
REVENGE OF THE BIGGS
77

Chapter 7
THE DIRECTOR'S CUT
90

Chapter 8
FRIDAY NIGHT LIGHTS
102

Chapter 9
SHOW TIME!
115

Chapter 10
CURTAIN CALL
126

CHAPTER 1

AT THE MOVIES

"You saved my life, but I don't even know your name."

"I am ... Slugwoman."

"WHOOOOOOOO!" yelled a voice. **"GO, SLUGWOMAN!"**

"Pan, be quiet," I hissed, clamping my fingers down on the jaw of the Mini-Dragon nestled among my popcorn. "They can't hear you—but everyone else can."

"SHHHHH," came a voice from behind us.

It was Saturday afternoon, and the MegaCinePlex was packed for the opening

weekend of the biggest movie of the year.
Slugwoman Begins was the eleventh movie
in the Slugman series. In order it goes:

SLUGMAN

SLUGMAN II: Return of the Slug

SLUGMAN III: Slug Hard

SLUGMAN IV: Slug Harder

SLUGMAN V: Slug to the Future

SLUGMAN VI: Planet of the Slugmen

SLUGMAN VII: Rise of the Slugman

SLUGMAN VIII: The Slugman Rises

SLUGMAN IX: The Slugman Rises Again

SLUGMAN X: Slug Wars (Parts 1, 2, 3,
4a, and 4b)

The movies had been getting worse and
worse ever since *Slugman III*, and the last few
were probably the most terrible movies I'd
ever seen. But now they'd rebooted the entire

series and changed Slugman to Slugwoman.
And it was genius.

"This is the best movie ever," declared Pan.

"It'd be even better if we could hear it,"
muttered Min.

"Yeah, Pan, you're going to get us kicked
out if you don't be quiet," whispered Jayden,
pointing toward a grumpy-looking teenage
boy named Kevin standing by the doors who
kept looking in our direction. We knew he
was named Kevin because all of the ushers
wore baseball caps with their
names on them.

"Slugwoman, if you don't figure out how to solve that cube puzzle in the next ten seconds, this whole spaceship is gonna blow!"

Nine seconds later, Pan let out a cheer. "I knew she'd do it!" he shouted. "Remember her dad, Major Slug, gave her a cube puzzle for her sixth birthday, right before he plunged to his doom down the salt mine. Of course, she's never been able to bring herself to try to solve it until now...."

"Yes, Pan, we know," I whispered. "We're watching it, too."

Suddenly, a light was shining on us. I quickly shoved Pan down into the bucket of popcorn.

"Hey, you three," said Kevin, pointing his flashlight directly in our faces. "Pipe down, or you're out of here."

"We're sorry," we said.

Kevin mumbled something under his breath before heading back down the steps.

"Pan, seriously!" I whispered.

"I'm sorry," he said, quietly this time.

This was the first time we had ever brought Pan to the movies—and almost definitely the first time a Mini-Dragon had ever been to one. We had figured there might be issues. There usually are with Pan. That's why we were sitting in the second row from the back, which had been as far up as we could get.

As an extra precaution, I'd bought the biggest tub of popcorn they had—the Colossus—to hide him in. He's only about six inches tall, so keeping him out of sight wasn't too hard. Keeping him quiet, on the other hand…. I had also hoped to eat some of the popcorn, but that was proving to be tricky.

According to the *Encyclopaedia Dragonica*, a huge book that contains everything you could ever want to know about dragons, Mini-Dragons' three main sources of food are mountain goats, prawn crackers, and dirty laundry. But thanks to my influence, Pan had started to expand his diet a bit. Okay, so we're only talking about marshmallows, but it was a start. And popcorn now, too.

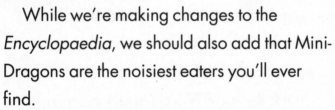

CRRuNNCH - CRRuNNCH!

While we're making changes to the *Encyclopaedia*, we should also add that Mini-Dragons are the noisiest eaters you'll ever find.

"If I can just figure out how this device works, I might be able to reverse the tractor beams."

"What device?" whispered Pan, hopping

around frantically in the tub. "I can't see what she's holding."

Of course, the problem with sitting near the back is that other people sit in front of you. Directly ahead of us were three tall men. It wasn't too bad for us non-Mini-Dragons, but Pan wasn't as lucky, even with me trying to position the tub so he could see through the gaps between them.

I was about to whisper a description of the device that Slugwoman was holding when I realized he wasn't there.

"Where's Pan?" I hissed, looking from Min to Jayden. They both gave me the same "Uh-oh" expression.

Seconds later, a couple of rows in front of us, a woman jumped up out of her seat.

"RAAAAAAAAAAAAAAT!"

Min, Jayden, and I let out a groan.

Kevin was up the stairs in seconds.

"I don't see anything," he said, scanning the floor with his flashlight. "Are you sure you didn't just—"

"Imagine it?" the woman snapped. "No, I did not. Come on, we're leaving this fleapit." She grabbed her boyfriend and dragged him out the door.

Seconds later, the "rat" reappeared.

"I got a better look at the device," whispered Pan, clambering up my leg and back into the tub. "It's the same as the one Potato Girl used in the opening scene. All Slugwoman has to do is tap it three times and—"

"Pan! I only agreed you could come if you promised not to run off," I said.

"But I was just—" he protested.

14

"Don't you remember the last time someone thought you were a rat?" interrupted Min.

"Miss Biggs busted up our entire classroom with a tennis racket trying to find you," said Jayden.

"Please, Pan," I whispered. "Just stay where you are, eat your popcorn, and watch the movie."

"Fine," sighed Pan.

We didn't hear a peep out of him for a long time after that—other than the crunching of popcorn. Eventually, though, there came a spluttering sound from inside the tub.

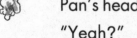 **CRRUNNCH - CRUNNCH - EWWW!**

Pan's head appeared over the top. "Eric?"

"Yeah?"

"What are these things?" Pan held up a handful of brown balls. "They're all hard, and they taste horrible."

"Oh, those are kernels," I whispered. "Popcorn that hasn't popped. You always get them at the bottom of the tub."

"Why didn't they pop?"

"Dunno." I shrugged. "Didn't get enough heat, I guess."

"Ah," said Pan. Then I realized what I had said. I looked down just in time to see Pan throwing a pile of kernels into the air, then blasting a short burst of flame at them.

The popcorn went everywhere.

"Hey, who threw that?" shouted a deep voice from a few rows in front of us. I slumped down in my seat, hoping not to be seen. But seconds later, a volley of popcorn was fired in our direction. The three of us ducked as it flew over our heads into the row behind us. A bunch of girls returned fire with a barrage of pretzel mix.

And then the call went up:

"FOOD FIGHT!"

It was like being in an action scene from the movie we were supposed to be watching. Hot-dog missiles shot past us, while strawberry gummy bears rained down everywhere. We ducked and dived, but nowhere was safe.

Then a flashlight was shining in our faces. "You three," snarled Kevin, brushing nachos from his cap. "Out."

"But the movie's almost finished," said
Jayden.

"Now!" barked Kevin, pulling a jalapeño
pepper out of his right ear.

"I can't believe we didn't get to see the ending," moaned Min as we shuffled through the foyer, shaking chips and cola-bottle candies from our clothes as we went.

"Yeah, thanks a lot, Pan," grumbled Jayden.

"I think you should say you're sorry," I said, looking down at the popcorn tub. "Pan... Pan?"

There wasn't much chance of an apology. Pan wasn't there. Again.

I spun around and was just about to tell the others when I saw the door to our screen open and some very angry, very messy-looking people emerge. And weaving between their feet, I spotted an upside-down cup.

I rushed over and scooped it up a split
second before the right foot of the huge man
who had been sitting in front of me landed
on top of it. The man gave me an odd look
as I grinned and hurried back to my friends.

"Pan," I said, quickly shoving him into
the pocket of my hoodie. "What were you
thinking? You could have been spotted."

"But I had to find out what happened," he
said.

AT THE MOVIES

"Must have been nice to see the ending," said Min.

"Yeah, thanks to you, we missed the big showdown between Slugwoman and the Red Empress," moaned Jayden.

"I'm sorry about that," said Pan. "I didn't realize popcorn was so … poppy. Anyway, you'll never believe it! At the end, it turns out that the Red Empress is actually Slugwoman's mom. How cool is that?"

Min, Jayden, and I stopped walking and turned to our left. A long line of people waiting for the next screening were staring at us with looks of horror.

"Spoiler alert!" shouted someone as mass booing broke out.

"I think we should go," said Min.

"Yep." I nodded.

We backed away slowly before turning and sprinting for the exit.

CHAPTER 2

CALLING ALL FILMMAKERS

Mom was waiting for us in the parking lot.
"Good movie?" she asked.

"Um ... yeah," I said, thinking of the parts
I'd actually seen.

"Any reason why there's a gummy bear in
your hair?"

I pulled it out and grinned as I held it
toward her. "For you," I said.

Mom laughed. "That's okay. I've just eaten."

We dropped off Min and Jayden and
headed home. Just as we pulled into the
driveway, it started pouring.

"Uh-oh, here we go," said Mom as we hurried into the house. "It's supposed to rain for the rest of the weekend, apparently. You're going to be stuck inside, I'm afraid."

But Pan and I didn't care. We spent the rest of the afternoon talking about the movie. Even though I hadn't watched the whole thing, *Slugwoman Begins* had still been the best movie I'd ever seen. We were still talking about it the next day.

"You know what would be great?" said Pan through a mouthful of prawn crackers as I returned to my room after lunch.

"To watch it again?" I suggested. "Maybe without so many interruptions. It might even be nice to see the end...."

"Well.... Yes, obviously," said Pan. "But I was going to say, wouldn't it be great to make a movie that good?"

"Us?" I said.

"Why not?" said Pan. "I bet Mini-Dragons are excellent at making movies."

Even though I knew it was far-fetched, a picture appeared in my head of the two of us sitting in our own director's chairs.

"That would be cool," I said. "What would our movie be about, though?"

Pan didn't hesitate. "Oh, that's easy. Picture the scene—a family of Mini-Dragons living peacefully in a mountain cave...."

"Uh-huh," I said. I had a feeling I knew where this was going.

"Then one day, their lives are turned upside down forever," continued Pan, "when EVIL property owners destroy their home. Forced to flee higher into the mountains, the parents must send their only son, the brave and handsome ... er ... Fan, to live with his cruel aunt and uncle in Mexico. Fan sails across the perilous ocean, fighting pirates and giant sea creatures. And then, in a twist of fate, Pan ... I mean Fan, ends up in the wrong country, delivered to a house in a box of bean sprouts ... no, a pizza box, where he befriends Eric—"

"Eric?" I interrupted.

"That's right," he said. "I'm naming him after you."

"Oh, well, thank you," I said, rolling my eyes.

"So Fan becomes friends with Eric and teaches him all sorts of important lessons and...."

"That all sounds very familiar," I said, giving him a wry smile. "Maybe we could have a scene where Fan gets dragon-napped or flushed down the toilet or smashes into tons of trees and ends up in a lake when he hasn't quite mastered flying. In fact, what if he uses a pair of underwear as a catapult to help with his takeoff? Yeah, I can see it now—a giant pair of computer-generated underpants."

Pan thought this over before emphatically shaking his head. "Nope. I don't like the sound of that at all."

CALLING ALL FILMMAKERS

We spent the rest of the afternoon scribbling down our fantastical movie ideas. By the time Mom called me for dinner, we had come up with a pretty strong list:

- **TOP DRAGON:** A hotshot young Mini-Dragon is sent to an elite academy for Dragon Flyers, where he trains to become the best of the best and gets to wear a leather jacket all the time.
- **ROBODRAGON:** Part Dragon. Part Machine. All Cop.
- **DRAGONS ON A PLANE:** Pretty self-explanatory.
- **SOME LIKE IT REALLY HOT:** Two Mini-Dragons go on the run from the mafia disguised as humans.
- **THE GOOD, THE BAD, AND THE MINI-DRAGON:** A western about a young cowboy who has to take the law into his own hands when a rival cowboy from a neighboring ranch steals his Mini-Dragon. Based on a true story.

"These are great ideas," said Pan. "Which one do you think we should go with?"

I let out a laugh but stopped when I realized Pan was serious.

"Oh, Pan ... we were just having fun," I said. "We couldn't actually make any of these."

"Why not?" he asked.

"Those kinds of movies cost millions," I said. "Even the awful ones."

Pan's smile drooped. "How are people expected to get that kind of money?"

"They get rich people to give them money," I said. "I heard Mom and Dad talking about it once. And then they go off and make a movie—the filmmakers I mean, not Mom and Dad. And when it gets released and people go to see it, the rich people get their money back. Unless no one goes."

Pan considered this for a few moments. "And you don't think we could get someone to give us millions of dollars to make a movie?" he asked.

"Unlikely," I said.

"Eric! Dinner's getting cold!" Mom called.

I left a disappointed Pan and hurried downstairs to the kitchen where Mom, Dad, and my little sister, Posy, were waiting for me at the table.

"Oh, here he is," said Dad as I sat down. "Not seen much of you today, Eric."

"I've just been hanging out in my room," I said.

"I hate it when it rains like this," said Mom as she put a plate down in front of me. I gazed at the sloppy mixture of browns and greens. Mom only makes decent food when my next-door neighbor Toby comes over for dinner. The rest of the time, we have to endure her "healthy" offerings. "You must be so bored, Eric."

I shook my head. "No, not really," I said. "We... I mean, *I've* been brainstorming movie ideas."

Mom and Dad exchanged surprised looks.

"Thinking of becoming a filmmaker, eh?" said Dad. "I like the sound of that. Make a few blockbusters, then send some of the cash our way. I could use it to sign Ronaldo for the Kickers."

"And I could teach yoga to the stars," said Mom.

"Not much chance of that," I sighed. "Unless you have a spare million I could borrow to get going?"

Dad took out his wallet and peered inside. "Nope, sorry," he said. "Guess the Kickers won't be winning any championships anytime soon."

Mom was just wiping a green smudge off the side of Posy's face when suddenly, she paused. Without saying a word, she rushed out of the room. I looked at Dad, but he just shrugged.

Mom reappeared seconds later, clutching

THERE'S A **DRAGON** IN MY **POPCORN!**

a pile of crumpled flyers.

"I always forget I have these," she said, dumping them onto the table. "Every time I teach my yoga classes at the community center, someone shoves a flyer into my hands. I hardly ever look at them, to be honest, but I just remembered noticing this the other day. I have a feeling it'll be right up your alley, Eric."

I took a purple one from the top of the pile.

"Tap dancing for beginners?" I asked, confused.

"What?" she said, snatching it out of my hand. "Whoops. Sorry, let me see.... Kayaking for couples.... Nope. Competitive Knitting.... No, not that one. How to make children eat anything.... I might hang onto that one myself. Ah, here it is!"

Mom handed me a yellow flyer.

COULD YOU

BE THE NEXT SPIELBERG?

ENTER OUR SHORT FILM COMPETITION!

 THEME: SUPERHEROES
AGES: 6-14

WE'RE LOOKING FOR BUDDING FILMMAKERS TO CREATE SHORT FILMS ABOUT SUPERHEROES. DON'T WORRY! THE MOVIES DON'T HAVE TO BE MADE ON A HUGE HOLLYWOOD-STYLE BUDGET—THEY CAN BE SHOT ON ANYTHING YOU LIKE, EVEN A SMARTPHONE! WE'RE LOOKING FOR MOVIES WITH HEART AND IMAGINATION!

ALL ENTRIES WILL BE SHOWN AT A SPECIAL SCREENING AT THE MEGACINEPLEX ON SATURDAY, OCTOBER 9

FOR DETAILS ON HOW TO ENTER PLEASE SEE THE BACK OF THIS FLYER!

THERE'S A DRAGON IN MY POPCORN!

I looked up at Mom. "Wow!" I said. "This looks amazing!"

"You could borrow one of our phones to film it on," said Dad.

"Thanks! That'd be great," I said. *Just wait until I tell Pan about this*, I thought. Then I reread the flyer. "Wait. The 9th? That's next Saturday."

"Oh, you're right," said Mom. "That flyer has probably been in my bag for a while."

"Do you think there's still time to enter?" I asked, remembering I had that thing called "school" that my parents insist I go to.

"It'll be tight," said Dad, "but I don't see why not. You can work on it when you get home from school next week."

I nodded. There was no time to waste. I got up and headed toward the doorway.

"Eric?" said Mom.

"Yeah?" I asked, stopping halfway out of the kitchen.

"Your dinner?"

"Um… I'm too excited to eat," I said, taking a final glance at the green mush on my plate.

Mom looked like she was about to tell me to sit back down, but then she sighed. "All right, go ahead."

"Thanks, Mom!" I shouted as I bolted upstairs with the flyer.

I burst into my bedroom with an excited look on my face.

Pan glanced up from the sheet of paper he was writing on. "What is it?" he asked.

I held up the flyer. As Pan read it, his eyes grew bigger with every line. Then he rolled up the piece of paper he had been working on into a ball, tossed it into the air, and shot out a small burst of flame, completely incinerating it.

"What was that?" I asked.

"*Dragons Are Forever,*" he said. "It was about a Mini-Dragon secret agent with a license to burn."

"Sounds good," I said.

"It was, but it wasn't a superhero movie," Pan said, cracking his tiny claws. "We've got a lot of work to do."

CHAPTER 3

EVERYDAY HEROES

"Wow, Eric!" said Min as we sat on a bench in the corner of the playground. It was morning recess, and I was showing her and Jayden the script for our movie: *Attack of the Cyber Kitty*. "Did you and Pan really write this whole thing last night?"

I nodded and let out a huge yawn. We'd had to scribble on a tiny notepad by flashlight under my comforter, just in case Mom or Dad came in. I was absolutely exhausted, but it had been worth it. We had a complete script for our movie. Now all we needed was the cast.

"This is good stuff," said Jayden. "Captain Cool rules with his laser-blaster shades. A superhero with a sense of style always gets my vote."

"Well, I like Einstein Girl," said Min. "She's smarter than the entire Internet."

"How did you and Pan come up with them?" asked Jayden.

I laughed at this, until I realized they both seemed to be expecting an answer.

"Isn't it obvious?" I said.

The pair shook their heads.

"They're based on you two!" I said.

Jayden frowned. "But I'm nothing like Einstein Girl."

"I think that might be me," laughed Min. "Well, that's very flattering, Eric, but why would you—"

"We were thinking you two could act in the movie," I interrupted.

"Us?" said Jayden. "Stars?"

"I've never acted before," said Min, looking unsure.

"That's why we wrote the characters based on you," I said. "Because then it won't really be acting. You can basically just be yourselves. Except in leotards," I added quietly.

Min still didn't look sold on the idea. "You know I don't actually know more than the Internet, right?" she said.

"See!" I said. "That's exactly the sort of thing Einstein Girl would come up with."

"And you really think I can portray someone as cool as Captain Cool?" asked Jayden, a bit too eagerly.

"Okay, now you're just fishing for compliments," I said. "So what do you say? Are you in?"

As soon as I got home from school, I hurried up to my room. "Pan, good news," I said. "Min and Jayden are on board."

"That's great," said Pan. "Especially since I just finished making their costumes. Turns out Mini-Dragons are excellent at costume-making."

Lying on my bed were two complete
superhero outfits. Captain Cool's was
a black one-piece with the letters CC
emblazoned on the front, and a silver cape.
Einstein Girl's was a long white lab coat
and wig of mad white hair. There wasn't a
leotard in sight!

"Awesome!" I said. But as I gave the costumes a closer look, something occurred to me. "Um, Pan, how did you make them?"

"Here are my designs," Pan said, handing me a sheet of paper.

"Thanks, but what I meant was … where did all the material come from?"

"Oh, I found some old fabric in a box in the spare room. There were all different colors," said Pan. "That's where I found the sewing machine, too. Took me a while to get the hang of it, but I think I did an okay job in the end. I also found an empty box for that other costume we needed—"

"Different colors?" I interrupted, racking my brain. Then I remembered. "Oh, you must have found Dad's old soccer jerseys. He changes the Kickers' colors every season because he thinks it'll help them play better. It never does. Anyway, Jayden and Min are coming over soon to start filming, so...."

"Tonight?" said Pan. "But isn't Monday the night that...."

DIIIIIIIIIING-DONGGGGG!

I let out a groan. How could I have forgotten? Tonight was the night Toby came over for dinner.

I watched as Toby chomped his way through a second helping of Mom's delicious chicken marsala, trying to decide how best to tell him I couldn't play video games tonight.

The last thing I wanted was for Toby to get wind of the movie competition. I couldn't imagine Min and Jayden giving their best performances with Toby hanging around laughing at them.

It would take some delicate wording to get away with this.

There would be no room for error.

Most importantly, though, it would require my parents to not blurt anything out.

"So, Eric, how's the movie coming along?" said Dad.

"What movie?" asked Toby.

"Eric's going to be a movie director," said Mom, beaming at me.

"Oh, really?" said Toby curiously.

"It's nothing," I said, getting up to put my plate in the dishwasher. "It's just this short film competition that's taking place on Saturday. It's nothing, really...."

"I wouldn't say that," said Dad. "I bet a lot of famous directors got their break in competitions just like this."

"He's right, you know," said Toby.

I waited for Toby to fire the first insult, but weirdly, it never came. Thinking about it, maybe it wasn't so strange. Ever since we had all gone camping together a couple of months ago, Toby had been a bit...nicer might be pushing things, but let's just say that the old Toby would have jumped at any chance to put me down. Don't get me wrong—he still insulted me plenty of times, but we're talking at least a twenty percent reduction.

"Well, Min and Jayden will be over in a minute to start filming," I said, heading for the kitchen door. "So if you want to play video games by yourself, Toby, that's fine with me."

"Can I come and watch?" he asked.

And there it was.

"Honestly, Toby, I don't think you'd—" I began.

"Of course you can," interrupted Mom. "Eric, maybe Toby can help. You were worried about not finishing it on time."

I shot Mom my best "ARE YOU KIDDING ME?" look, but Mom always seems to confuse that with my "WHAT A GREAT IDEA, MOM!" look.

"Excellent. That settles it, then," she said. "Here, take my phone."

I took Mom's cell phone and we went into the hallway only to find our path blocked by our cat, Patches. She was struggling to free herself from a large silver box decorated with an assortment of lights, dials, and wires— clearly another creation of Pan's. Cool though the costume was, I was more impressed by the fact that he'd managed to get it on Patches.

Toby looked at me in confusion.

"The movie is called *Attack of the Cyber Kitty*," I explained. "Anyway, we're filming in the backyard. I'll meet you out there in a minute—I just need to go and get the script." Of course, I was going to get Pan, too, but given Toby's habit of trying to steal what he thought was a hi-tech dragon toy, I left that part out.

"Don't worry, Crispo," he said as I was halfway up the stairs. "I promise I won't get in the way. You won't even know I'm here."

CHAPTER 4
TOBY OR NOT TOBY

"I'm not doing it with him watching," said Jayden, pointing at Toby, who was sitting over in the corner of the patio in a chair.

"Look, he promises he's not going to laugh or anything," I said, trying my best to sound convincing.

"And Toby would never break his promise," muttered Pan, hiding in the neck of my hoodie.

"Pan agrees," I said.

"I was being sarcastic, Eric," said Pan.

"Oh," I said. "Well, look, other people

are going to see it eventually, so what does it matter if he watches now?"

"All right," said Min, frowning. "Let's get this over with."

It wasn't quite the level of enthusiasm I was hoping for from my cast on the first day of filming. And after I had even gone to the trouble of organizing a special trailer for them to get changed in.

"That's just your shed," Jayden had said when I pointed it out to them.

"You're actors now," said Pan. "Just pretend it's a trailer."

I'm not sure Min and Jayden had appreciated Pan's comment, but they'd taken turns to step inside the shed and change into their costumes.

And as Einstein Girl and Captain Cool, they looked great. Well, great considering the outfits were made in a day by a Mini-Dragon.

Slowly we turned toward Toby, expecting to
be knocked over by his laughter.

But he didn't say a word. Instead, he
smiled encouragingly and gave us a thumbs
up. The three of us exchanged puzzled
looks. At least when Toby was being rude,
you knew where you stood.

"Come on," insisted Pan. "We've only got about an hour's light for filming."

"Where do you want us?" asked Jayden.

"Um … over there, I guess," I said, pointing toward the fence behind them. "Now, let's take it from the top."

"Eric?" shouted Toby.

I shook my head. "Yes, Toby?"

"No, it's nothing," he said. "It's just…. Well, wouldn't you be better filming from the other side of your yard, by the tree?"

"Um … why?" I asked.

"Well, the sun's on that side," he replied. "But if you stood over by the tree to film, it'd be behind you."

"Okay, thanks, Toby," I said, rolling my eyes. "The sun! Can you believe it?"

There was a pause before anyone spoke.

"I hate to say it, Eric," said Pan, "but I think he might be right."

"Yeah, it does make sense," said Min. "The light should be shining on the actors, not into the camera."

I looked around the yard. "Fine, let's move it over there, then."

As Min and Jayden got in position, I pulled out Mom's phone and switched the camera on. Or tried to anyway.

"Press that," said Pan, pointing at the bottom of the screen. I quickly turned my back to Toby so he wouldn't see the Mini-Dragon showing me how to use the phone.

"This?" I asked.

"No, not that one," said Pan.

"Oh, you mean this?"

"No.... Now you're calling Aunt

Ruth. Okay, the one to the left...."

At last, the camera app appeared on-screen.

"Now, slide that to switch it to video mode.... Good job!" said Pan, giving me a withering look.

"What?" I said. "I don't have a phone, remember."

I held up the phone toward Min and Jayden, making sure they were both in the shot. "Ready? Action!"

Captain Cool: Einstein Girl, you felt the tremors, too?

Einstein Girl: Indeed, Captain Cool. I left the lab at once.

Captain Cool: You think it's Dr. Hideous up to his old tricks again?

Einstein Girl: I can't say for certain. But what I am sure of is that the world is in great danger.

Captain Cool: Wait, what's—?

"Hang on, guys," I interrupted. "I don't think it was actually recording. Can we try again?"

"Come on, Eric," said Jayden. "I was acting my shades off there."

"I'm sorry," I said.

"Do you want me to press the button?" asked Pan, a little too patronizingly for my liking.

"No, I've got it," I said. "And ... action!"

Min and Jayden repeated their lines, then continued on with the script.

Captain Cool: Wait, what's that over there, in the distance?

Einstein Girl: I can't see anything.

Captain Cool: Hang on. I'll use my Tritanium shades to get a better look. They let me see great distances, you know.

Einstein Girl: Yes, I invented them,

remember?

Captain Cool *(pulling down his glasses):* Oh, yes, I forgot. Let me see now…. Oh, no! It's worse than we could ever have imagined!

Einstein Girl: What is it?

Captain Cool: It's … it's … it's—

"Um…. I'm sorry, guys," I said, cutting them off. "Don't hate me, but it looks like I've had the camera turned the wrong way around. I've been filming my nose the whole time."

If looks could kill, I'd at least be seriously injured by the glares Min and Jayden were giving me.

"So unprofessional…," muttered Min.

"How are we expected to work under these conditions!" mumbled Jayden.

"Don't worry," I said. "I'll get it this time. You guys were great, by the way. Pan, how do I…?"

Pan sighed as I held up the phone, making sure to turn away from Toby again. "You press this button to switch the view…," he said, his voice trailing off. "Oh, Eric, that looks horrible."

"It's just my nose," I said, feeling a little self-conscious.

"No, not that," said Pan. "Look at the video quality."

Pan was right. Mom's phone wasn't exactly state of the art. The footage of my nose was all grainy.

"Well, it's not like we have any other choice," I said. "I'm sure Dad's phone is even older than this one. Maybe there's a way to make it better."

"Everything all right, Crispo?" shouted Toby.

"Yes, fine, thank you," I lied. "Just trying to find the picture-quality setting."

Toby stood up and began walking toward us. I gave Pan a little nudge, and he popped back down into my hood.

"Yeah, your mom's got the X3 model," said Toby. "I had that one when I was four. The camera's pretty basic. That's as good as it gets."

"Really?" I said, my heart sinking.

"'Fraid so," said Toby. "It's fine for the odd selfie, but you're not going to impress anyone shooting a movie on that. You know, I could always…. No, I'm sorry, never mind. I'll go back to my chair."

As Toby walked away, I couldn't stop myself. "What were you going to say?" I asked.

Toby stopped. "Well, it's just…. If you needed help…."

"What kind of help?" I said slowly.

"Well, I can fix the camera situation for starters," he said. "I can get you cameras like the pros use."

"How?"

Toby tapped his nose. "Mom and Dad have connections," he said. "Don't you worry about it."

I knew there had to be a catch. With Toby, there always was.

"And what do you want in return?" I asked.

Toby pretended to look offended. "Eric, I'm hurt that you would even suggest.... But now that you mention it, I suppose I could get a credit on the movie. Nothing major.... Producer, maybe?"

"Nothing major?" laughed Min. "A producer is one of the biggest credits there is."

"Well, I would be helping make the movie better," said Toby defensively. "Though of course I'll be strictly hands-off. This is Eric's project, after all, and I wouldn't want to interfere with that. What do you say, Eric?"

As much as I knew better than to trust Toby, it was tempting. With better equipment, we could make a better movie and….

"OWW!" I shouted as a tiny pair of claws jabbed me in the neck.

"Ow?" repeated Toby as everyone stared at me.

"Um… H-Oww … about I go over there and think about it?" I said, pointing to the corner of the yard.

Toby looked at me as if I had gone crazy but gave a shrug. "Sure, whatever you need to do, Crispo."

I headed off across the yard, keeping my back to the others.

"What did you jab me for?" I asked Pan.

"You can't seriously be considering working with Toby," he said furiously.

"It might not be that bad," I said.

"It's Toby!" said Pan.

"I know," I said. "And that's a good point. But you said it yourself. Mom's phone is garbage. Now, if we want to make something anywhere near as cool as *Slugwoman*…."

"Yes…. BUT TOBY?" said Pan.

"Look, it's like I told you, Pan," I said.

"This is what professional filmmakers do. They get people to invest in their projects. But the filmmakers still get to make the movies they want to make. This is the same thing. We'll have control, but we'll get decent equipment, and all we have to do is put Toby's name on the credits. It's a business deal, Pan. Anyway, I really think Toby might have changed since we went camping," I added. "He's not anywhere near as mean as he used to be. Last week, I accidentally beat him at a video game, and he didn't try to get me in trouble. He just went home instead."

Pan didn't look convinced. "Look…," he said. "For the record, I think this is a terrible idea. But if you really want to do it, then … I'm with you."

"Thanks, Pan," I said. "It'll all work out, trust me."

Ignoring the glares Min and Jayden were giving me, I walked back over to Toby and stuck out my hand. "All right, Toby," I said. "It's a deal."

Toby gave me a smile that sent a shudder down my spine. "You know it makes sense," he said. "Leave it to me. In the meantime, if you can e-mail me a copy of the script, that would be great. Just so I know what it is I'm funding."

"But it's handwritten," I said. Claw-written, too, but I didn't mention that.

"Shouldn't take you long to type it up," said Toby as he walked away. "It's not like you're doing much else now, right? See ya."

"I've still got a bad feeling about this," said Pan.

CHAPTER 5

WHO WANTS TO BE A STAR?

"So how's the movie going?" asked Mom as we drove home from school the next day.

"We haven't actually gotten any footage yet," I admitted. "But Toby's arranging for a new camera for us, so hopefully we should get something shot this afternoon."

"Oh, that's nice of him. I'm glad you're letting him be involved," she said.

"Well, I wouldn't use the word 'involved,'" I pointed out. "Because he's not going to...."

My voice trailed off as we turned onto our street. Outside Toby's house was a huge line of people stretching all the way up the road and around the corner into his backyard.

"What in the world...?" said Mom as she pulled into our driveway.

I leaped out of the car and rushed up the stairs to find Pan pressed up against my bedroom window, staring out at Toby's backyard.

"What's going on?" I asked.

"It's Toby," said Pan. "He's auditioning people."

"He's doing *what*?" I said. "But we've already got our cast."

"You'd better get down there and tell Toby that," said Pan.

I changed out of my uniform, shoved Pan into the pocket of my hoodie, and dashed back downstairs and out the front door.

"Hey, no jumping the line!" shouted a muscular guy in a white T-shirt at least two sizes too small for him as I squeezed past.

"I'm the director," I said.

The guy's face turned a little pink. "Oh, I'm so sorry," he said. "Stand aside, everyone, director coming through. Stand aside!"

Suddenly, people were practically jumping out of the way to let me past. I quickly reached the front of the line, where Toby was sitting at a wooden table.

"You call that acting?" shouted Toby at a boy with floppy blond hair. "You've got about as much charisma as a brick."

"Toby, what are you doing?" I asked.

Toby's face lit up. "Ah, Crispo, you're here. You should have heard the garbage that was coming from this one. Didn't make a bit of sense."

"I was reciting Shakespeare," said the boy.

Toby rolled his eyes. "Never heard of her," he said. "Next."

As the boy walked away shaking his head, I repeated the question. "Toby, what are you *doing*? What are all these people here for?"

Toby looked at the huge line, then back at me. "Well, it's an audition, isn't it?"

"Yes," I said. "I can see that. But why are you having one? We already have a cast."

"Oh, your friends?" asked Toby. "Jin and Maiden, wasn't it?"

"Min and Jayden," I corrected. "You saw them last night. And we all went camping together—you know who they are!"

"Right, right," said Toby, looking completely uninterested. "Great guys. So they're actually going to be in the movie, then? Oh, okay. Still, there are more than two characters in the script. What were you going to do, have them play all the roles?"

I scratched the back of my head. "Well … yeah."

Toby shook his head in dismay. "Oh, Crispo," he said. "It's a good thing you brought me on board."

"I brought you on board?" I asked.

"Best decision you've made yet," he said. "Here, take a seat. We've got a lot of people to get through. I got in touch with

all the local amateur drama clubs offering
their members the chance to star in a major
motion picture."

"So you lied?" I said.

"No such things as lies in the movie
business, Crispo," said Toby, leaning back in
his chair. "Only opportunities."

"Can't we just get on with the filming?" I
asked.

"The camera doesn't arrive until
tomorrow," said Toby. "Which is good
because it gives us time to assemble the best
cast we can."

I let out a sigh. But since there was nothing
else I could do, I sat down next to him.

"What's going on?" hissed Pan, half an
hour later.

"Not much," I whispered back. "Some

of them are good, but Toby's rejecting everyone."

"Isn't that your job?" asked Pan.

"Well, yeah, but...."

"Did you say something, Crispo?" asked Toby.

"No," I lied. "Listen, Toby, how much longer do you think this will take?"

Toby shrugged. "Who knows? But if it takes us all night to find the perfect Innocent Bystanders one, two, and three, then so be it."

I still didn't see why we couldn't just have Min and Jayden play those parts, too.

"Oh, no," I said, leaping up. "I should have called Min and Jayden to tell them not to bother coming over."

"Isn't that them over there?" asked Toby, pointing toward the end of the line. Sure enough, there were my two lead actors, waving at me and looking extremely annoyed.

"You go, Crispo," said Toby. "I'll handle things here."

"What's going on?" asked Min as I hurried over.

"Toby's decided to hold an audition," I explained.

"For our roles?" asked Jayden, looking hurt.

"No, no," I said, trying to calm them down. "For the extra characters."

"Hang on, you said Toby decided?" said Min. "But it's your movie."

"I know, I know," I said. "But he's kind of right.... It might look a bit weird if you're both playing a bunch of characters. Plus, it's less work for you this way."

"Okay," said Jayden. "So when do we start filming?"

"Tomorrow, for sure," I said, trying to sound confident.

"Eric, you're not going to let Toby take over, are you?" asked Min in a weary voice.

"Of course not. Anyway," I said, attempting to change the subject, "what are you two doing in the line? You guys don't have to audition."

"This muscly guy in a tiny white T-shirt wouldn't let us past," said Jayden. "We've been trying to get your attention forever."

"Sorry about tha…," I said, my voice trailing off as I looked back to where Toby was sitting. Three huge boys were standing beside him, laughing. I recognized them as Toby's friends from school—Big Ricky, Big Quinn, and Big Joey.

"No way," Pan muttered as I started walking toward them.

"Oh, Eric, you're back," said Toby. "Good news! I've found us our three Innocent Bystanders."

"Those three?" I said. There was nothing innocent about them. "You've got to be joking, Toby."

"You should have seen their auditions," said Toby. "All three were Oscar-worthy."

As the three goons pretended to look bashful, Toby suddenly looked away, distracted. I followed his gaze. Standing at the front of the line was the last person I ever expected to see—a giant woman with curly white hair and the meanest of faces.

"Miss Biggs!" I cried, almost falling over at the sight of my teacher.

"Miss Biggs?" repeated Pan.

"Crisp?" she said, looking just as surprised to see me. "What are you doing here?"

"This…. This is my neighbor's house," I said. "This is my audition. Um, what are *you* doing here?"

"*Your* audition?" she said, looking horrified. "Well, as it turns out, as well as being the finest teacher in the country, I'm also one of its best actors. In 1978, I played the lead role in a stage production of *A*

WHO WANTS TO BE A STAR?

Streetcar Named Desire."

"You played a car?" said Toby, looking confused.

Miss Biggs's nosed flared a little. "No, you silly boy. I was Blanche DuBois. And I was phenomenal. Now if someone can get me a script, I'll let you know which of the main characters I'll be playing."

I could feel the color draining from my face. How on earth could I tell her that I didn't want her in the movie? She hated me enough as it was.

As it turns out, I didn't have to tell her. My "producer" decided to handle it himself.

"Sorry, lady," said Toby. "All the roles have been filled. Isn't that right, Eric?"

I looked at Toby's brainless friends. I didn't want them in the movie. But I *definitely* didn't want Miss Biggs in it.

"That's right," I muttered.

"There, see," said Toby.

Miss Biggs looked ready to explode. She shot me a Biggs Death Stare like I had never seen before. After a few seconds—which felt like hours—she turned around and walked away.

But as she reached the gate, she paused for a moment and looked back at me. "See you at school tomorrow, Crisp," she said through the thinnest of smiles.

"Well, that's not going to be good," whispered Pan.

CHAPTER 6
REVENGE OF THE BIGGS

I spent the next day at school trying to avoid giving Miss Biggs an excuse to punish me for not casting her in the movie. I just wanted to keep my head down, but she kept firing questions at me, trying to trip me up.

"Crisp! What's eleven times fourteen?"

"Um… a hundred and fifty-four?"

"What's the capital of Peru?"

"Um… Lima?"

"When was the Battle of Hastings?"

"1066?"

Somehow, I made it to the end of the

day without slipping up. I figured this was because of two things:

1. Having a friend as smart as Min to give me the answers.

2. Being surprisingly good at lip-reading.

Foolishly, as the bell rang, I thought I was home free.

"Crisp, wait," barked Miss Biggs as the rest of the class left the room.

"Yes, Miss Biggs?" I said.

"Sit down," she said, pulling up a chair next to her desk.

I did as I was told.

Miss Biggs opened a drawer and took out a large brown paper bag. Her eyes locked with mine as she slowly opened the bag.

"Candy?" she asked, holding the paper bag out to me.

Candy? What kind of mind game was this? I peered inside. Sure enough, it looked to contain a handful of hard candies in all different fruit flavors. There was only one possible explanation—they had to be poisoned. I shook my head.

Miss Biggs looked confused for a moment. Then it seemed to dawn on her that I might not trust her.

"Oh, for heaven's sake," she said, rolling her eyes. She took out a red ball and popped it into her mouth. "See, it's fine," she mumbled. "Take one."

Still no wiser about what was going on, I took a green one.

"There," she said. "This is nice, isn't it?"

No, I thought.

"Yes," I said.

We sat there for almost fifteen minutes, just eating candy. Miss Biggs offered no explanation as to why I was there, and I was too scared to ask. I didn't seem to be in trouble, but every time I tried to leave, she would insist that I take another. I was halfway through a purple ball when Mom burst into the room.

"Eric!" she cried. "What's going on? I've been waiting in the car forever. Miss Biggs, is Eric in trouble?"

Miss Biggs made the same surprised face she had given me earlier. "Trouble?" she said. "Oh, certainly not. On the contrary, Mrs. Crisp," she said, gesturing at the bag of candy. "Eric is being rewarded for his outstanding performance today."

Mom screwed up her face. "Eric? Outstanding?"

"Thanks, Mom," I said, frowning.

"What? Oh, I'm sorry, Eric. What I meant was...."

"He got every answer right today," said Miss Biggs. *"All by himself."* She gave me a knowing look as she said this.

"That's great. Fantastic job," said Mom. "It's just that the traffic gets really bad if we don't leave on time. And there's a lot of construction at the moment, too. It's going to take us forever to get home now."

"Oh, no, I'm sorry," said Miss Biggs. "Well, you must get going, then. And good luck with your movie on Saturday, Eric."

So she knew about the competition?

"He's not going to have much time to film the thing if we don't get back soon," said Mom as she led me out of the classroom.

I could tell from the smirk on Miss Biggs's face that she knew that, too.

The traffic was so bad that it took us almost an hour to get home. Min and Jayden were waiting for me on the doorstep, and neither of them looked very happy. From the muffled sound coming from Min's pocket, I had a feeling Pan wasn't happy, either.

"I'm sorry, guys," said Mom. "Eric was

held up at school. You haven't been here long, have you?"

They both shook their heads, but I suspected from the glares I was getting that that probably wasn't true.

"Do you mind if I skip dinner, Mom?" I asked as she opened the front door. "I'm still full from all that candy."

Mom sighed. "Okay, but you're having something decent to eat later."

"Candy? Where have you been?" asked Jayden once Mom was inside. He had a panicked look on his face.

"I got stuck at school," I said, not wanting to go into it. "What's wrong?"

"It's Toby," said Pan, popping his head out of Min's pocket. "He went over to Evergreen Park to start filming with his friends."

"Filming?" I repeated. "As in *our* movie?"

They all nodded.

I could feel my blood starting to boil.
"Let's go," I said.

Evergreen Park is pretty large. Which is
great when you need a quiet, out-of-the-
way spot to help train a Mini-Dragon to
fly, but not so great when you have to find

someone in a hurry. We eventually tracked down Toby in the kids' play area. He was standing in front of a wooden pirate ship, pointing an expensive-looking video camera up at it, while Big Ricky held a boom. On the bow of the ship was Big Joey. He was holding on to Big Quinn, who had his arms outstretched as if they were wings.

Big Quinn: I'm flying.

Big Joey: No you're not. This is how you fly!

Big Joey gave Big Quinn a shove. I gasped as Big Quinn went soaring off the top of the pirate ship, landing in a crumpled heap on the ground. But instead of screaming in agony like a normal person, he burst out laughing—as did Toby and Big Ricky, who were watching from the side.

"Cut!" shouted Toby. "That was perfect. Who needs stunt doubles?"

"Toby, what's going on?" I shouted.

"Ah, Eric, you made it," said Toby. "Wait until you see the footage we've got. Solid gold."

I hardly knew where to begin. "You

started filming without us?"

"Well, I didn't know how long you'd be, did I?" said Toby. "And the deadline is in three days so I thought, *Well, I've got the camera, I can get things started for you.*"

"Get started how?" I asked. "You didn't even have Min and Jayden. They're the stars."

Toby nodded thoughtfully. "Yeah, that was a problem," he said. "But they insisted on waiting for you. Luckily, I had three great actors on hand."

Min, Jayden, and I looked around.

"Where?" asked Min.

"He means us," grunted Big Ricky. "Umm…. You do mean us, don't you, Tobes?"

"Tobes?" laughed Jayden.

"Of course I mean you," said Toby, ignoring Jayden. "Honestly, Eric, wait until you see the footage. They're really good."

"Let me get this straight, Toby," I said.

"You've filmed your friends as Captain Cool and Einstein Girl?"

"Of course not," Toby laughed. "They wouldn't fit in the costumes, for starters. No, I just had to beef up the Innocent Bystander roles a little, that's all."

"Beef them up? Well, can I see the footage?" I asked.

Toby glanced at his watch. "Actually, I promised Mom I'd … um … clean my room. So I'd better get back home."

I knew for a fact that Toby's family had a housekeeper who did that. But if Toby was heading off, then that was fine with me. "No problem," I said. "Just leave the camera with me."

Toby shook his head. "No can do, Crispo," he said. "The insurance on this thing means I've got to be present at all times. Besides, it's getting dark now. You'll never be able to film anything in this light."

"I thought we had a deal," I said. "You supply the equipment, and I make the movie."

"Look, let's not argue," said Toby. "We'll meet up tomorrow and you can film the rest. In the meantime, you might want to take another look at your script. With the changes I had to make for the guys, I don't think Captain Einstein and Cool Girl are going to fit anymore. I think you might need to write your friends some new roles if you still want them in the movie."

"New roles?" said Min.

"Exactly!" said Toby, already halfway across the play area. "See you at my house tomorrow!"

We stood there in stunned silence, until Pan stuck his head out of my pocket. "Am I the only one who doesn't remember there being a pirate ship in our script?" he asked.

CHAPTER 7
THE DIRECTOR'S CUT

Pan and I stayed up late again that night, rewriting the script. Min and Jayden had made us promise to come up with even better parts for them than before. But how were we supposed to do that when we didn't even know what changes Toby had made? We didn't have much of a choice, though. If we left it to the following day, we'd run out of time. Speaking of school, I couldn't stop worrying about the thought of getting another "reward" from Miss Biggs and being late getting home again.

But then something completely unexpected happened. Miss Biggs called in sick!

Substitute teacher days were always cause for celebration in our class, but for me, it was even sweeter. I was out of the school gates in record time. Mom drove Min and Jayden home with us, and Dad had burgers waiting for everyone. There was no way Toby was going to be able to pull anything today.

"You ready, Pan?" I asked through a mouthful of burger as I entered my bedroom.

Pan was scribbling notes on the paper in front of him. "Yep," he said, looking up. "I've been making tweaks to the script all day. Not to brag, but this might be the best thing anyone's ever written."

"*Not* to brag?" I laughed, picking up the script and flicking through it. "Actually, some of this is really good. But we better hurry if we want to get it filmed tonight."

"Right," agreed Pan, climbing up my leg and into my jeans pocket.

Down in the kitchen, I showed Min and Jayden the script.

"So we're supposed to learn all these new lines in the next five minutes?" asked Jayden.

"If you could, yes," I said.

"It shouldn't be too bad," said Pan. "I've tried to write the dialogue the way you guys speak so it's easier for you to remember."

Min looked at the script and frowned. "I would never say 'Get your claws off my planet, you no-good space critter.'"

"You might if there was a space critter nearby," reasoned Pan.

We headed over to Toby's house. Just as I was about to ring the bell, the front door sprung open, and a thin man wearing a flat cap pushed past us. He was quickly followed by about a dozen other people, carrying all sorts of weird and wonderful things including:

- Three fancy ballgowns
- Half a dozen laser guns
- A life-size inflatable skeleton
- A jewel-encrusted electric guitar
- Several cacti with human faces
- A scarecrow wearing a tuxedo
- A Labrador puppy

- A large spinning wheel, like you'd find on a TV game show
- Two huge pythons—one real, one fake
- A pair of giant fluffy dice

At the back of the line was Toby.

"Ah, Crispo, you're just in time," he said.

"Just in time for what?" I asked. "And who were all those people?"

"Eric, I woke up this morning in a panic," said Toby, sounding overly dramatic. "*It's Thursday*, I thought. *We don't have much time left, and our movie is looking terrible.*"

"*Our* movie?" I repeated.

"And the script," continued Toby. "I'm sorry, Eric, but I'm just not feeling it anymore."

"We have a new script," I said, holding up the pile of paper.

"You bet we do," said Toby. "Wait until you see what the scriptwriters I hired have come up with."

"Scriptwriters?" said Min. "As in ... professionals?"

Toby nodded. "That's right. These guys have come up with a script so good that not only will we win the competition, I think we've got a shot at an Oscar, too. You want to see it?"

"The script?" I said. "No, Toby, not really. I've got—"

"No, not the script," he said, cutting me off.
"The movie. Do you want to see the movie?"

Min and Jayden let out gasps.

I placed my hand on my jeans pocket to
stop Pan from launching himself at Toby.

"I'm sorry, Toby," I said in a quiet voice.
"I must have misheard you. I thought you just
asked if I wanted to see the movie."

"That's right!" Toby grinned. "It's all
done. I knew we weren't going to have time
to realize my … I mean, *our* vision, so Mom
let me take the day off from school to work
on it. I had to hire tons of people to help—
that was them all just leaving—but we got
there in the end. Come on. Let's watch it."

I was too stunned to shout or scream or
do anything except follow Toby upstairs
to his bedroom, which was now filled with
expensive-looking computers.

"Okay, ladies and gentlemen, boys and

girls," boomed Toby. "I give you *Titanic Wars: Revenge of the Dinosaur King.*"

"What kind of title is that?" asked Jayden.

"If you want a movie to be successful, you have to know what works," said Toby. "So I just went through the movies that made the most money and borrowed parts from them."

Toby hit a button on a keyboard, and the screen of his laptop went black. The opening credits appeared:

TITANIC WARS:
Revenge of the Dinosaur King.
A TOBY BLOOM PRODUCTION
A few weeks ago, in a galaxy not that far away—in fact, it's this one....
It is a time of really bad peril. A new ship called the *Titanic* has been built. It's really cool and has all the best laser guns and can fly into space and go underwater.
But some evil dudes want to steal it.

"Enough," I said, heading for the door. "Toby, I want nothing to do with this movie."

Toby sat back in his chair and smiled. "Ah, but you haven't had anything to do with it, have you, Crispo?"

"What are you talking about?" I fumed. "It was my idea in the first place."

"Right," he said. "But you haven't actually done anything. You haven't even touched a camera. Your friends aren't in any scenes, and not a single thing you've written has made it into the movie. Seems to me like this is my movie, not yours."

I could tell by how much I was having to press down on my pocket to contain Pan that, had he gotten out, we'd have had one very toasted Toby standing in front of us.

"I suppose there's always time to make your own movie," Toby laughed. "In two days, on your mom's garbage phone."

98

"This was your plan all along, wasn't it?" I said. "To stop me from making a movie while you made yours."

Toby gave me a slow clap. "Well done, Crispo. You got there in the end. Everyone knows real filmmakers are ruthless. That's why I've got what it takes and you don't. It's a pity you didn't want to watch it now. You'll just have to line up with everyone else on Saturday to tell me how amazing it is. With all the professionals I hired, there's no chance I won't win. Now, if you'll kindly get lost, I've got a few finishing touches I need to make to MY movie."

"Well, it sounds like trash," muttered Jayden as we left.

"You won't be saying that when I win an Oscar!" shouted Toby.

"I can't believe Toby," said Min when we got outside.

"Why, because he's normally so nice?" said Jayden.

"Fair point," said Min.

"We're not going to let him get away with this, are we, Eric?" asked Pan, hopping down from my pocket and pacing my front lawn. "We can still make our own movie. We'll just shoot it on your mom's phone the way we were going to before *he* got involved."

I shook my head. "We've been over this, Pan," I said. "The camera's no good."

"So what?" said Pan. "This was just meant to be fun. And at least we'll get to make it our way."

"No," I said firmly. "Toby's right. There isn't enough time. He outsmarted us, Pan, and there's nothing we can do about it."

"We've got today and tomorrow," said Jayden. "There's still a little bit of light."

"And I could always ask my mom if we could borrow her phone," said Min.

"No. There's no point," I said firmly.

As much as I appreciated my friends' support, I had already wasted everyone's time getting duped by Toby. There was no point in wasting even more, trying to pretend we could possibly make a movie from scratch. "I'll see you guys tomorrow," I mumbled. "Come on, Pan."

Without another word, I walked back into the house.

CHAPTER 8
FRIDAY NIGHT LIGHTS

Pan wouldn't let it drop. He spent the rest of the night trying to convince me to do it. He was still at it the following morning.

He badgered me while I brushed my teeth. He pestered me as I packed my school bag. He even hid in my cereal.

"For the last time, we're not making the movie," I said, keeping my voice down so my parents wouldn't hear.

I pushed my cereal bowl aside and took a slice of toast instead.

"How's the movie coming along, Eric?" asked Dad. "All ready for tomorrow?"

"No," I said. "I'm not entering anymore."

"Oh, that's a shame," said Mom. "You seemed so excited at the start of the week."

"Yeah.... Well, it didn't work out."

I ate the rest of my breakfast in silence.

"Well, we'd all better get going," said Mom, getting to her feet.

"Not me," said Dad. "There's a problem with the lights at the stadium. The electrician is fixing them, so we've had to move practice to tonight. Gives me time to draw up some fresh tactics for our next game."

"Oh, okay," said Mom. "Well, we'll see you later, then. Come on, Eric."

Even Miss Biggs being out again couldn't
cheer me up. As I shuffled over to my desk,
I could hardly look at Min and Jayden,
knowing how badly I had let them down.
Thankfully, neither of them made any mention
of the movie the entire day. All I wanted to do
was put the whole thing behind me.

   After school, Mom was waiting at the
gate, which was a little unusual as normally
she stayed in the car. Before I could ask her
why she was there, she waved at Min and
Jayden to come over.

"Hello, you two," she said. "You're staying with us tonight."

"We are?" said Min and Jayden in unison.

"I've spoken to your parents and gathered overnight bags for you both," she said before turning on her heel and hurrying back to the car.

"What's going on?" I asked as the three of us followed her. Then I noticed my sister wasn't in her car seat. In fact, the car seat was missing altogether. "Where's Posy?"

"Aunt Ruth is taking her for the night," said Mom. "We've got work to do."

"Work?" I said as the three of us piled inside.

"That's right," said Mom, starting the car.

As we pulled out into the street, I looked over my shoulder. "This isn't the way home," I said, even more confused.

Mom smiled at me in the rear-view mirror. "Who said anything about going home?"

She refused to say another word about where we were going. Finally, we turned into a small parking lot that I knew well.

"The Kickers' stadium?" I groaned. "We're not going to watch them play, are we?"

"She did say we had work to do," said Jayden. "I guess she meant it."

"Come on," said Mom, opening the car door.

Min and Jayden got out, and I was about to do the same when I felt something pinch my bottom.

"Ow," I said. "I think I sat on something."

"You did," whispered a voice. "Me. About ten minutes ago, when you got in."

"Pan?" I said, looking down. There, wedged between the seats, was one very

squished Mini-Dragon.
Carefully, I reached
into the gap and
pulled him out.

"What were
you doing
there?" I asked.

"Hurting mostly,"
he said, straightening
his crumpled wings.

"No, I mean, why were you in the car in
the first place?" I said.

Pan grinned, but before he could tell me
what he was up to, Mom shouted, "Are you
coming, Eric?"

I gave Pan a frown before putting him in
the pocket of my coat. "Coming," I said.

Min turned to me, wide-eyed. "That
wasn't Pan, was it?" she whispered.

"Yep," I said.

I followed Mom into the stadium and out onto the pitch, where Dad and the rest of the Kickers were running in and out of orange cones. As soon as Dad spotted me, he broke away from the others and came over.

"Hi, Eric," he said. "You ready?"

I squinted at him suspiciously. "Ready for what?"

"To finish your movie!" he said.

"My movie? What are you talking about?" I said.

"Technically, he'd have to actually start the movie first," muttered Min.

"Well, your mom and I read your script, and—"

"You read my script?" I interrupted.

"You did leave it lying on top of the box I keep my game notes in," said Dad. "And I told you I'd be working on them this morning, so you must have wanted me to look at it. I showed your mom when she got back."

That wasn't right. I knew for a fact that last night I had dumped the script in the corner of my bedroom, in a pile with the costumes and Patches's robo-suit. I hadn't been able to bring myself to throw it out. But how could the script have ended up in the kitchen?

Of course. Pan. I looked down at my coat pocket and could just make out Pan's face, smiling up at me apologetically.

"We have to say, Eric, it's really good," said Mom. "I know you told us you were done, but your dad and I think you should reconsider."

"You ... really think it's good?" I said.

Mom and Dad nodded.

It was nice that they liked it, but I realized it didn't change anything. "We don't have enough time," I said.

"Nonsense," said Mom. "We'll all stay

up as long as it takes to get it finished."

"Yeah!" said Min and Jayden.

"But it's going to be dark soon," I said.

Dad had a puzzled expression on his face. "Have you forgotten you set your movie in a soccer stadium?"

A soccer stadium? "There's no soccer stadium in the script," I said.

"Sure there is," Dad said, still looking a little confused as he reached into his sports bag. He pulled out a stack of paper and handed it to me.

I quickly skimmed through the script. It was more or less the original version, except for a few notable changes. One of which was that the story now took place in a soccer stadium. I looked down at Pan, who was still grinning at me.

"I guess I did forget," I said. "But what difference does it make, anyway?"

Dad laughed. "Are you kidding?" he asked. "We can do this for starters."

Dad put his thumb and index finger in his mouth and let out an ear-piercing whistle. Seconds later, the entire pitch was lit up as if it were the middle of the afternoon.

The floodlights!

"And I've had a word with the boys," said Dad. "They're all up for being extras in the movie if you need them."

"Their acting can't be worse than their playing," whispered Jayden.

My mouth was hanging open. Maybe, just maybe, this could work. Except there was still the issue of….

"Oh, and I almost forgot the best part," said Dad as if reading my mind. "Our goalie has a camera we use to film our games every week. You can use that."

"What do you think, Eric?" asked Min.

"Yeah, are we doing this or what?"
said Jayden.

I nodded. "We're doing this."

As everyone let out a cheer, Dad
pointed at a suitcase on the ground.
"We brought your costumes," he said.

"The only thing we didn't bring was Patches."

"You know she hates traveling in the car," said Mom.

"Not as much as she hates being dressed in a box," added Dad.

Gears started turning in my head. I ran back to the car and opened my school bag.

"You're not mad at me, are you?" said Pan. "It was just this morning when I heard your dad talking about practice, I thought—"

"Oh, I'm not mad," I said, pulling out my gym shorts.

"What do you need them for?" he asked.

"You'll see," I said. "Normally I'd use a pair of underwear, but I didn't bring any spares. Now, I just need to make a few more changes to the script...."

CHAPTER 9
SHOW TIME!

"Eric?"

"Eric?"

WHAACK!

WHAACK!

WHAACK!

"Owww!" I cried, rubbing my eyes as I lifted my head off the keyboard of the laptop. "Pan, why are you slapping my face with my slipper?"

"Because my hands are too small," he replied.

"No, that's
not what I....
Why are you
slapping me
at all?"

"Because
we're going to be late
for the screening!" shouted Pan.

"Ugh," moaned Jayden, who was lying
facedown on top of my bed, still in his
Captain Cool costume. "What's Pan shouting
for?"

"He says we're going to be late," I said.

"What time does it start again?" yawned
Min from her sleeping bag.

"Ten," said Pan.

"And what time is it now?" asked Jayden.

I looked at my watch. "Well, that can't be
right," I said.

Suddenly, I was fully awake. "We've got

to go!" I shouted. "We're supposed to be there in fifteen minutes."

As Min and Jayden slowly woke up, I rushed out of the room. There was no sign that Mom and Dad were up yet, either, so I banged on their door.

"We need to get going," I cried. "Now!"

Filming had gone on late into the night. When we finally got home, everyone else had gone right to bed, but Pan and I had stayed up and used the laptop to make all our footage into a proper movie.

Luckily, Mini-Dragons are excellent at video editing. At some point, I must have nodded off. I couldn't even remember if we'd finished it or not.

I ran back to my room. "Pan, the movie— is it ready?" I asked.

Pan rolled his eyes. "Of course it is," he said. "While you were busy sleeping, I was putting the finishing touches on it. I even burned a copy for you."

Min and Jayden exchanged worried glances.

"When you say burned…," began Min.

"On to DVD," said Pan, holding up a shiny disc and giving Min another eye-roll.

"Well, to be fair, you are a dragon," said Jayden. "You can understand her concern."

"I want everyone dressed and in the car in five," called Mom as she headed downstairs. "Toast will be provided. Do *not* leave crumbs in my car. Everyone clear? Good."

Mom's commands were obeyed to the letter (except for the part about toast crumbs). Unfortunately, there was still construction, and it took us half an hour to get to the MegaCinePlex.

We burst through the cinema doors, and the woman at the ticket desk waved us through. But as we hurried toward screen one, a familiar teenage boy stepped in front of us. It was Kevin, the usher who had thrown us out of *Slugwoman*.

"Here for the movie competition?" he sneered, folding his arms. "Well, you're too late."

"Surely it can't be finished yet," said Dad.

"It's not," agreed Kevin. "But the deadline has gone by. No exceptions."

"Oh, enough, Kevin." A small, balding man wearing a fancy-looking tuxedo and holding a gigantic tub of popcorn walked over. "What's the harm in letting them in?"

"But Mr. Graham, sir," whined Kevin.

"I've told you before, my name is Harry."

Ignoring Kevin's protests, Harry turned to us. "Which one of you is the entrant?" he asked.

I raised my hand.

"And your name is?"

"Eric," I said. "Eric Crisp."

"Crisp, huh? Well, how about that. We're only up to the Bs. The kid before you is still going. He started about twenty minutes ago. I came out to stretch my legs and grabbed some popcorn while I was at it."

I glanced at Min and Jayden. "His last name isn't Bloom by any chance, is it?"

"Bloom? Yes, that's it. He obviously missed the part about these being *short* films. I told Margaret, the other judge, that we should have put a time limit on the flyers. I knew this would happen. Well, you'd better give me your entry, Eric. Please tell me it's not long."

"It's about five minutes," I said, handing him the DVD.

"Perfect," Harry said. "Go on in."

We walked past a seething Kevin into the darkened theater and were immediately greeted with one of the most disturbing sights any of us had ever seen. A twenty-foot-high image of Toby's head wearing a crown.

"I AM THE DINOSAUR KING, AND I WILL HAVE MY REVENGE, IN THIS LIFE OR THE NEXT. BUT PROBABLY THIS ONE!" he boomed.

"Wait," Pan whispered from my jeans pocket. "He cast himself in the movie, too?"

"Are you really surprised?" I asked.

We headed for the back row to watch the rest of Toby's movie. Any worries we had about being late seemed silly by the time the thing finally ended, an hour and a half later.

"It didn't even make any sense," said Jayden. "Why would dinosaurs be on the *Titanic*, anyway?"

SHOW TIME!

"And the part where Toby chopped off the heads of those three pirates," said Min. "Were they supposed to be us?"

"They were named Min, Jayden, and Eric," Jayden replied. "So probably, yeah."

"Well, at least he remembered our names for once," said Min.

Toby's movie had everything. And I don't mean that as a compliment. It almost literally had everything. There were:

- pirates from the future

- The *Titanic*

- A fight between snakes and clowns

- Seven different kinds of alien

- Talking dinosaurs with attitude

- Two car chases, with dozens of explosions

- A musical number involving Big Ricky, Big Joey, and Big Quinn (which was surprisingly good)

When it finally ended, there was a collective sigh from the audience. Well, from those who were still awake, anyway.

"Ahem ... yes," stammered a woman I assumed was Margaret as the lights came back on. Like Harry, she had dressed for the occasion, wearing a long blue gown and heels. Neither of the judges would have looked out of place on a Hollywood red carpet. "That was ... *Titanic Wars: Revenge of the Dinosaur King*, by Toby Bloom. And it was very ... um ... very...."

She looked at Harry for the right word.

"Long?" he suggested.

"Ambitious," she said. "It was very ambitious. A round of applause for Toby."

A grinning Toby stood up and took a bow as everyone clapped politely. "If I can just say a few words about my art—" he started.

"Moving on," continued Margaret, cutting him off. "Next up, we have Eric Crisp and his movie—*Pitch Invasion*."

Just as the lights dimmed, I caught a glimpse of Toby's face turning purple with rage.

CHAPTER 10
CURTAIN CALL

A nervous-looking goalkeeper appears on screen.

Facing him, a man stands in front of a soccer ball, poised to take a penalty kick.

Suddenly, the player looks up past the keeper, his eyes wide with fright. He's pointing at something. The keeper shakes his head, thinking it's some kind of trick to distract him. But then the other players start pointing and screaming, and then:

"ROOAAAAAAAARRR!"

CURTAIN CALL

The keeper turns around
and sees a giant dragon
soaring above them,
breathing fire.

As the players run
for their lives, a boy
with a silver cape
and a girl wearing
a lab coat step into view.

Goalkeeper: It's Captain Cool and Einstein
Girl. They'll save us!

Captain Cool: A dragon? Not cool. I'll
use my laser-blaster shades against it.

Einstein Girl: They won't be any use
against a dragon's thick skin. But if we can fire
something into its mouth at exactly the right
speed and angle, it might be enough to block
his windpipe and prevent him from using his
fire breath. We'd need something small and
round....

Captain Cool: Like a soccer ball, you mean?

Einstein Girl: Precisely. But we'd need someone skilled enough to kick it into the beast's mouth.

Right on cue, Dad appears wearing his Kickers soccer jersey and a mask we made by cutting eyeholes in a bandage from his first-aid box.

The Kicker: Did someone say they needed a soccer ball kicked?

Captain Cool: Yes, we did. Just a second ago.

Einstein Girl: The Kicker! Do you think you can make the shot?

The Kicker: No problem.

The Kicker takes aim but then appears to panic.

Captain Cool: What's wrong?

The Kicker: I'm too nervous. What if I screw up?

Einstein Girl: He needs to relax. If only he were as cool as you, Captain Cool.

"I can't believe Jayden made us put that line in," whispered Pan.

Then Mom steps forward, wearing her yoga clothes.

Yoga Woman: Did someone say they needed to relax?

Captain Cool: Yes! Seriously, do all superheroes just wait around until someone says something that applies to them?

Yoga Woman closes her eyes, puts her hands together, and balances on one leg. The screen goes all hazy, then confidence seems to flow through the Kicker, and he whacks the ball skyward.

In slow motion, the ball rockets toward the dragon, whose mouth is wide open like a goal as it prepares to let out another blast of flame. The ball lodges itself in the beast's throat, and the dragon tumbles to the ground as our heroes roar in triumph. All the soccer players rush back onto the pitch and lift The Kicker and Yoga Woman in the air as the end credits play.

The lights came back up, and there was a thunderous round of applause. Even Big Joey, Big Quinn, and Big Ricky were clapping, until they noticed the foul look Toby was giving them.

"Well, that was fun," said Margaret.

"Agreed," said Harry. "And it was short, too."

"That was fantastic, Eric," said Mom. "You know, maybe I should give up the yoga and become an actor instead. I wasn't half bad."

CURTAIN CALL

"How did you manage to do that part with the dragon flying and breathing fire?" asked Dad, leaning over.

I had expected my parents to ask this, so I had a response ready.

"On the computer," I said, glancing down at my jeans pocket.

Visibly impressed, Dad nodded as though the answer had been obvious.

In truth, here's my director's guide to having a dragon in your movie:

1. Hire a Mini-Dragon. They're much easier to work with than your larger variety.

2. Zoom in close when he's flying so that he looks huge.

3. If he has trouble taking off, a pair of underwear can be a good makeshift catapult to help him get airborne. Gym shorts will also do the trick.

4. Give him a smartphone to take with him so he can also do some filming while he's up there.

5. Make sure no one sees your dragon by instructing the rest of your cast to look in the opposite direction and pretending you're filming them instead.

The biggest problem was Pan's landing. He still hasn't quite gotten those perfected yet. Luckily, no Mini-Dragons were harmed during the making of this production. Maybe he was a little bruised, but Pan has had worse.

"Next up," said Harry, taking a DVD from the top of the pile in front of him, "we have *Bat Teacher* by…. Hey, how did this get here again? All right, where is she?"

Harry scanned the crowd and pointed toward the back row. "You! How did you get in?" he shouted. "I told you, this competition is for kids aged six to fourteen."

I couldn't believe it. Sitting in the back row, trying her best not to be noticed, was Miss Biggs. She was wearing shorts and a T-shirt, and her white hair was straining to escape a backward baseball cap.

"Um … yo, dude," she said in a squeaky voice. "I'm totally, like, fourteen and stuff."

"Someone go get Kevin," sighed Margaret.

"Fine!" snapped Miss Biggs in her regular voice, standing up. "It's your loss, though. My movie is a masterpiece, much better than all this other junk."

Miss Biggs stormed out to roaring laughter, flinging her baseball cap at a baffled Kevin.

"So that's why she was off the last couple of days," said Jayden.

As we watched the rest of the entries, Pan and I were unable to wipe the smiles off our faces. We'd shown our movie, and people had actually liked it! Some of the movies were really good, and by the time the last one played, I was pretty sure we couldn't possibly win. But I didn't care in the slightest. I was just so glad that the others had convinced me to enter. Seeing our finished movie up there on-screen was all the reward I needed.

Then the moment came—the awards'
announcement.

"The runner-up prize," began Margaret,
"for what we felt was the most inventive film in
the competition, goes to—Eric Crisp!"

Runner up! I could hardly believe it. I got
another huge round of applause as I went
up to collect a small silver trophy.

"Would you like to say a few words?"
asked Harry.

"Um ... sure," I said, not really knowing what to say. I had barely had time to finish the movie, let alone come up with an acceptance speech. "I guess I need to thank my parents for convincing me to make the movie and also for starring in it. And my friends Min and Jayden for all their hard work and, well, for putting up with me. And big thanks to the Kickers for all their support. And—oh, yeah—I'd like to thank the little voice that's always in my head. This is as much his award as it is mine."

There was silence, and I realized everyone was staring at me.

"How ... inspirational," said Margaret, sounding slightly baffled. "Great job, Eric."

As I walked back to my seat, I saw Toby sneering at me.

"I couldn't have done it without you guys," I said, sitting down next to my beaming parents and friends. I lowered my voice to a whisper. "I definitely couldn't have done it without you, Pan."

"Well, obviously," said Pan, grinning up at me from my pocket.

"And now the winner," said Harry. "For a movie that reduced us all to tears...."

Toby had already stood up and was walking toward the stage.

"Samantha Armstrong for her moving story about what happens when teenage superheroes leave school and need to find jobs—*Power Park Rangers*."

A girl jumped up from her seat and shot past a stunned Toby.

Suddenly, there was a loud bang behind us as the doors burst open. Standing there was a large, wild-eyed man, his hair shooting off in all directions like he'd been trying to pull it out.

"D-D-Dad?" stammered Toby. "What are you doing here?"

"I'm here because of *this*," said Mr. Bloom, holding up a sheet of paper.

"What's that?" asked Toby.

"This, son, is my credit card statement," he snapped.

"Oh," gulped Toby. "Well, you did say it was okay to use—"

"I *said* you could buy a video camera and some props! This is top-of-the-line stuff I've paid for. Not to mention scriptwriters, extras, catering, costumes, video editing, and an orchestra! Get in the car *now*. This is coming out of your allowance."

As a gloomy-looking Toby was marched out by his dad, the entire room burst out laughing.

The following day, Pan and I were already at work on the sequel.

"What about a horror movie, with an evil Mini-Dragon aunt and uncle? Or a tense

thriller with a baseball-bat wielding Mini-
Dragon hunter? Or—"

"It'll be Christmas soon," I said. "What
about a Mini-Dragon Christmas story?"

"I like it," said Pan.

"Great," I said. "Let's open up the laptop
and get started."

"Yeah—and I'll be able to check out how
we're doing," said Pan.

"What do you mean 'how we're doing?'"
I asked.

Pan went silent, realizing he had said
something he shouldn't. "Um…. Promise you
won't get mad?"

I closed my eyes. "I'm not promising
anything," I said. "What have you done?"

"Well…. I might have accidentally posted
our movie online," he said.

I didn't reply at first. I wasn't mad. I didn't
really know how I felt. I thought about people

140

CURTAIN CALL

from all over the world being able to see and comment on our movie. I guess I was nervous.

"Let's take a look," I said. Pan signed into the account he had set up, and we opened the video. I headed right to the comments.

MrPotato 10 mins ago

Wow, that was awesome!!! Keep up the good work.

Doug45 15 mins ago

LOVE IT!

JulieD 16 mins ago

Please make more!

TobesB 18 mins ago

Worst thing I've ever seen. If you guys want to see a good movie check out *Titanic Wars: Revenge of the Dinosaur King* by this guy named Toby Bloom. He's a genius.

Other than that last comment, which we had our suspicions about, everyone seemed to be raving about our movie. Then I scrolled back up and saw the number of people who had viewed it. My mouth dropped open. It was more than a hundred thousand.

"Wow!" I said.

"I only posted it last night," said Pan. "Well, this changes everything."

"What do you mean?" I said.

"I'm famous now," declared Pan. "So I'm going to need to be paid. A million—no, two million prawn crackers, I think. And I'll need my own trailer, naturally."

"Where are you going?" I asked as he wandered off.

"I need to speak to Min and Jayden," he said. "See if they want to be my agent and bodyguard. Oh, but I can't go out looking like this. Eric, will you be a dear and see if your mom has any cream I can use for my cracked skin?"

"Cut!" I shouted. "CUUUUUUUUUTTTTT!"

Hungry for more?
Find out how Eric met Pan in:

CHAPTER 1
A CHANGE OF FORTUNE

"Hey, Eric," said the tiny short-haired girl standing outside my front door. Min Song and I were in the same class at school, but right now she was here on official business, which was why she was carrying a dozen Chinese takeout boxes under her chin. "I'm sorry we're so late."

"Um … we ordered five minutes ago," I said, checking my watch.

"I know, I know, but traffic was a nightmare," she said, nodding toward her dad, who was sitting on a moped with the words "Panda Cottage" emblazoned on the side, impatiently tapping his watch.

"No, what I meant was—" But before I could finish, Min had shoved the huge pile of boxes into my arms.

Then she picked up a box that had fallen to the ground. "Oh, and don't forget your bean sprouts."

"Bean sprouts?" I said, looking puzzled. "I don't think we ordered—"

"No, they're free," interrupted Min. "We have way too many of them. Please, just take it."

"Oh, okay," I said. "You know, I've never actually tried them."

"You'll love them. Probably. Anyway, I have to go."

I put down the boxes and handed her the money, before she hopped on the moped and it disappeared down the road.

"Min took her time!"

That's my dad, Monty Crisp. He's the reason we were having Friday-night Chinese. My dad coaches the local soccer team, the Kickers, and we were celebrating their latest success—a final score of 10–1.

"I still can't believe it," he said as I handed him the boxes. "We got an actual goal. First time in five years. All right, so technically it was the other team that scored it for us, but our own goal still counts!"

I'm sorry—I should have been more clear: They *lost* 10–1.

The Kickers are the worst soccer team of all time. In their 50-year history they've only ever won a single game, and even then it was because the other team had to forfeit after getting stuck in traffic.

"You should be very proud, dear," said my mom, Maya. In case you're wondering, her legs are currently over her head because she's a yoga instructor, not because she's weird.

Though she is weird.

Mom unfolded herself and joined me, Dad, my two-and-a-half-year-old sister, Posy, and our horrible, definitely evil cat, Patches, at the kitchen table.

Half an hour later, the Crisp family was officially stuffed, as you can see from my helpful diagram:

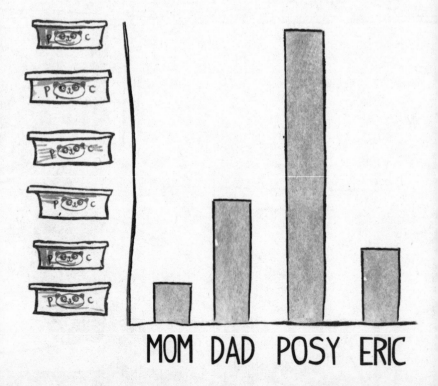

MOM DAD POSY ERIC

The number of boxes for Posy is misleading. Those are the number of actual boxes she attempted to eat. She doesn't care about the food; she just loves chewing plastic.

After dinner, Dad was back talking sports.

"All I'm saying, Eric," he said, reaching for the fortune cookies, "is that it wouldn't kill you to take an interest in athletic pursuits. Like soccer or tennis or…."

"Yoga?" suggested Mom.

"Be serious, Maya," said Dad. "Um…. I mean…."

Mom glared at him. "I'll pretend I didn't hear that."

Dad mimed wiping sweat off his brow. "Phew. But really, Eric, it was only last week you told me you thought offside was when only *one* side of the bread had gotten moldy…."

"He was *teasing*, Monty," said Mom. "You

were teasing him, weren't you, Eric?"

Before I could reply, Dad cut in: "Hey, would you look at that?"

He held up a small piece of paper.

VICTORY WILL BE YOURS

"Amazing!" cried Dad. "It's destiny."

I rolled my eyes. "Everyone knows fortune cookies are junk, Dad. The last one I got said 'Your shoes will make you happy.'"

"And did they?" Dad asked.

"Not that I noticed...."

"What did you get this time, Eric?" asked Mom.

I cracked open the shell and unfurled the piece of paper inside.

YOUR LIFE IS ABOUT TO CHANGE

"Hmm. Well, you do turn nine soon," Mom said.

"A week tomorrow," I reminded her. She *probably* knew that already, but my birthday was WAY too important to take any chances with.

"Ooh, look at mine," said Mom. "'Your son will handle the cleaning up.'"

"It doesn't say that," I said.

"Well, all right," she admitted. "It's actually the same as Dad's."

VICTORY WILL BE YOURS

"But your cleaning up will be a nice victory for me," she said.

I let out a groan, but I knew from experience that I had about as much chance of getting out of it as the Kickers did of winning, well ... anything.

I rinsed out all the boxes and took them outside. I'd almost finished putting them in the recycling bin when I realized that the box of bean sprouts was still unopened.

Even though I was stuffed, I was curious to find out what they tasted like. I opened the lid and jumped back in fright. Not because of the bean sprouts, though they didn't look that appetizing, but because nestled inside the box was a small green scaly object. It had:

A long dragon-like snout.

A long dragon-like tail.

Big dragon-like wings.

Sharp dragon-like teeth.

Short dragon-like arms and legs.

Dragon-like claws.

There was no doubt about it. Whatever it was looked a lot like a dragon. Its tiny, marble-like black eyes seemed to stare back at me and, for the briefest of moments, I almost convinced myself it was real.

Ha. A real dragon. Can you imagine?

Was Panda Cottage giving out free toys with their food now?

"Snappy Meals," I said out loud, before remembering there was no one around to laugh at my joke.

I took the toy out of the box and was surprised by how it felt. Whatever it was made of, it wasn't plastic. I once touched a

lizard at the zoo and it felt similar—rough
and cool to the touch—but this was much,
much harder. It really was the most lifelike
toy I had ever seen. It must have taken
forever to paint. Not that it even looked or
felt painted, mind you. It was too realistic.
Every scale was a different shade of green,
with small, freckle-like flecks of yellow
across the snout. Gently, I moved its arms
and legs back and forth, feeling a little
resistance as I did so, almost as if it didn't
appreciate me doing it.

Whoever had made it must have gone to
some trouble—way more than a free Chinese
takeout toy was worth, that's for sure.

After trying a handful of bean sprouts
and deciding I wasn't a fan, I shoved the
dragon into my pocket, went back inside,
and headed upstairs. After all, it was
Friday, and I had a lot to do. My comics

weren't going to read themselves.

I put the tiny dragon on a shelf before diving onto my bed and settling into issue #437 of my favorite comic: *Slug Man*.

A short while later, Slug Man was just about to take a call from the police commissioner on the Slug Phone when I felt something tugging at my pant leg.

ABOUT THE AUTHOR

Tom Nicoll has been writing since he w in school, where he enjoyed trying to fi as much silliness in his essays as he coul possibly get away with. When not writin he enjoys playing video games (especiall the ones where he gets beaten by kids ha his age from all over the world). He is als a big comedy, TV, and movie nerd. Tom lives just outside Edinburgh, Scotland, wi his wife and two daughters.

ABOUT THE ILLUSTRATOR

Sarah Horne grew up in Derbyshire, England, and spent much of her childhood scampering in the nearby fields with a few goats. An illustrator for more than 15 years, she started her illustration career working freelance for newspapers and magazines. When not at her desk, Sarah loves running, painting, photography, cooking, movies, and a good stomp up a hill. She can currently be found giggling under some paper in her London studio.